THE INFINITY RAINBOW CLUB

CONNOR AND THE TAEKWONDO TOURNAMENT

BY **JEN MALIA**

ILLUSTRATED BY **PETER FRANCIS**

beaming ☀ books

MINNEAPOLIS

For my husband, Dave, who made it possible for me to write this series, and Spyro, Leslie, Clayton, and Pho, who taught me everything I know about Taekwondo—JM

To all those that inspire and nurture the best in ourselves—PF

30 29 28 27 26 25 24 23   1 2 3 4 5 6 7 8 9

Hardcover ISBN: 978-1-5064-8599-7
Paperback ISBN: 978-1-5064-9652-8
eBook ISBN: 978-1-5064-8600-0

Library of Congress Cataloging-in-Publication Data

Names: Malia, Jen, author. | Francis, Peter (Illustrator), illustrator.
Title: Connor and the taekwondo tournament / by Jen Malia ; illustrated by
    Peter Francis.
Description: Minneapolis : Beaming Books, 2024. | Series: The infinity
    rainbow club ; 3 | Audience: Ages 7-10. | Summary: When Connor's rival
    joins his Taekwondo team, he must find a way to stay focused for the
    upcoming tournament.
Identifiers: LCCN 2023019495 (print) | LCCN 2023019496 (ebook) | ISBN
    9781506485997 (hardback) | ISBN 9781506496528 (paperback) | ISBN
    9781506486000 (ebook)
Subjects: CYAC: Attention-deficit hyperactivity disorder—Fiction. | Tae
    kwon do—Fiction. | Friendship—Fiction.
Classification: LCC PZ7.1.M34696 (print) | LCC PZ7.1.M34696 (ebook) | DDC
    [Fic]—dc23
LC record available at https://lccn.loc.gov/2023019495
LC ebook record available at https://lccn.loc.gov/2023019496

Beaming Books
PO Box 1209
Minneapolis, MN 55440-1209
Beamingbooks.com

Printed in China.

CHAPTER 1

Not in a million years did Connor Stark think he would be sparring with his nemesis, Wyatt. On Saturday morning, they were in Master Park's Taekwondo *dojang*. It was where Connor had trained and fought in sparring matches for the past five years. He had started learning Taekwondo when he was only four.

On the walls hung Korean and American flags and murals with the five tenets of Taekwondo: courtesy, integrity, perseverance, self-control, and indomitable spirit. The tenets were written in English and Korean Hangul script.

In the middle of the floor, interlocking blue foam squares formed two large sparring rings. Around the blue squares, red foam squares covered the rest of the floor. Connor and Wyatt stood inside one of the large blue squares on opposite ends of it.

Today was his first Taekwondo class of the new year. And Connor was really looking forward to *kyeorugi*. Sparring was his favorite part of Taekwondo. Connor had a red belt with a black stripe taped on the end. He was one step away from a junior black belt, or *poom*. He usually fought teammates one rank below him, the red belts, because no one else in his class had his rank. Except Wyatt was a red belt with a black stripe too. But he wasn't supposed to be in Master Park's dojang.

Connor's Taekwondo team was the Lions. At tournaments, their biggest rival was the Titans—Wyatt's team. Connor had sparred with Wyatt in tournaments ever since starting Taekwondo. Sometimes Connor won, and sometimes he lost. Connor would never say it out loud, but he knew they were equally matched.

When Connor showed up in the dojang that morning, he got the worst news ever. Wyatt had moved over winter break and wanted to be a Lion. And that meant Connor would have to see Wyatt in his Taekwondo class *three* times a week! But Connor knew one thing for certain—Wyatt was *not* a Lion. *Once a Titan, always a Titan*, thought Connor.

Haley refereed the match. She was a *poom* and assisted Master Park in the dojang. Haley was also the big sister of Connor's best friend, Nick. Haley pointed to the center of the ring. "Chung!" she said in Korean. It meant *blue*.

Wyatt moved as commanded. He wore his *hogu* on the blue side. The chest protector wrapped around his body and tied in the back like a really big laced-up shoe.

Haley pointed to a spot across from Wyatt. "Hong!"

Connor moved to the center of the ring. He wore his hogu on the red side.

Connor and Wyatt stood face-to-face in their *dobok*, or white uniforms. They wore full sparring gear that included chest, hand, and arm protectors, shin and foot protectors, and mouthguards. Their belts poked out under their hogus. And their foam headgear was tucked under their left arms.

"Charyeot," Haley said.

Connor and Wyatt stood at attention with their arms straight by their sides.

"Kyeong-nye," she said.

They bowed, facing each other. And they put on their headgear.

Haley lunged forward with her left leg. Her open hand near her ear chopped down between Connor and Wyatt. "Junbi!" Haley left her hand there until Connor and Wyatt were ready.

They got into fighting stance. Connor and Wyatt bounced on the balls of their feet with one leg in front

of the other. Their fists were up, ready to protect their heads or block lower shots to the body. Connor had 90 seconds to show Wyatt that he was the better fighter.

Haley slid her left leg backward. She put both of her hands together like she was about to clap. "Shijak!" And the match started.

Wyatt danced around Connor on the balls of his feet. He put one leg in front. Then the other. Every time Wyatt changed legs, Connor switched too.

Like a lion hunting, Master Park watched Connor and Wyatt from outside the ring. The Lions was the perfect team name. Master Park's first name, Saja, meant *lion* in Korean. She was a fourth-degree black belt who had won a gold medal in Taekwondo.

Connor made the first move. *Dollyeo-chagi*, a roundhouse kick. He lifted his right leg with his knee pointed at the target and pivoted on his left foot. His right foot whipped around with the top of it aimed at Wyatt's hogu. "Hi-YAH!"

Wyatt slid back on his feet. Connor had kicked air. *Not* Wyatt's hogu. Connor landed right in front of Wyatt.

"KYA!" Wyatt punched the middle of Connor's hogu. "KYA!" Wyatt landed dollyeo-chagi on the side of Connor's hogu. The punch wasn't powerful enough to score a point. But the roundhouse kick put Wyatt in the lead with two points.

Connor couldn't believe he had let Wyatt get him first. He should've been ready for the counterattack. But Connor knew he had to forget about getting hit and stay focused.

The rest of the round was a blur. Switches. Punches. Kicks. Wyatt blocked every move Connor made. And Connor blocked everything that Wyatt tried too. But Connor saw an opening after he blocked Wyatt's side kick. Connor landed dollyeo-chagi on Wyatt's hogu. And just like that, Connor tied up the match at two.

The class cheering sounded like a roar. The bright lights overhead blinded Connor. And he couldn't stop replaying in his head the last time he had fought Wyatt in a tournament. They had been tied up near the end of the match. And Wyatt had sprained his ankle trying to land *dwi-chagi*. Wyatt's back kick had hit air when Connor moved out of the way. Wyatt twisted his ankle when he fell to the ground. Connor had won by forfeit. But the match felt like an unfinished fight rather than a win.

Focus on this match, Connor told himself. *Naeryeo-chagi to the head is my best shot.* An axe kick to the head was worth three points. And he wanted to go for the win.

The round was almost over. *It's now or never*, thought Connor. He sucked in air. Sweat beaded up on his forehead. He was just about to strike Wyatt with an axe kick to the head. But out of the corner of his eye, Connor saw Wyatt's foot come up toward the side of his head.

Protect your head, Master Park always said. Connor's fists were already up near his head. His left forearm was right where it needed to be to knock Wyatt's foot away.

Connor started to throw up his arm in a high block to protect his head.

"KYA!" Wyatt yelled.

But Connor was too late.

Thunk!

CHAPTER 2

When Wyatt's foot hit Connor's head, the dojang looked
like it had tilted. Connor lifted his head back up. The
training room went back to normal. And time was up. The
match was over. And Connor couldn't believe it. *What
just happened?* Connor wondered. *Why couldn't I block
the kick?*

Wyatt got three points for landing *nakka-chagi* on
Connor's head. Wyatt didn't hit Connor hard with the
hook kick. Just a tap to the head with his heel to show
that he got him. Wyatt won the match five to two.

Wyatt extended his right hand toward Connor for a
handshake. Wyatt's left hand was palm down under his
right elbow. The traditional Taekwondo handshake. The
last thing Connor wanted to do was shake hands with his
archenemy.

But Master Park had taught him to always show
respect in the dojang. And that meant shaking hands
with an opponent no matter how the match went. Connor
looked Wyatt in the eye while shaking hands with him.

Like Wyatt, Connor put his open hand under his elbow. Master Park had said an open hand showed your opponent that you weren't carrying a weapon. At least, that was the way it was back when the tradition started.

Connor left the ring and sat cross-legged on the floor next to his younger brother, Luke. The sparring matches started with the highest-ranked belts. The next round started between two red belts.

"Whoa," Luke whispered to Connor. "Are you okay?"

"I don't want to talk about it," Connor whispered back.

Master Park always said to focus on the match and nothing else. *Why couldn't I do that?* wondered Connor. But he knew why. Losing focus was always the reason

Connor froze up in a sparring match. It wasn't that he couldn't focus on a fight. He was really good at sparring. At least, he *was* really good at it before today. But sometimes the noise, the lights, and his thoughts were too much to handle. Having Wyatt suddenly appear in his dojang was a huge distraction.

Connor had attention deficit hyperactivity disorder. Luke had ADHD too. And their dad had it. Connor had wondered what the chances were for him, Luke, and Dad to all have ADHD. Dad had said it runs in families, and the odds were very good. For Connor, ADHD meant that he often lost his focus, moved around a lot, and acted without thinking first.

Connor's head hung low.

"It was just one round," his friend Violet whispered into his ear. She sat cross-legged on a red square next to him. "I know sparring is your thing. But you'll get another chance." Violet was in fourth grade at Deer Park Elementary like Connor. But they weren't in the same class.

"I guess so," Connor whispered back. He was disappointed with himself. *How could I freeze up like that?* thought Connor. *Especially in front of Wyatt?*

Violet was new to Taekwondo and didn't know what mistakes Connor had made in the match. Mistakes a red belt with a black stripe shouldn't have made. She was a white belt, the lowest rank in Taekwondo. Two months ago, Violet had decided she wanted to try a new sport because exercise helped calm her mind and body. She was less anxious when she kept moving. Connor had told Violet about Taekwondo. And she had joined. He was happy to have another friend on his team. But he wished he hadn't lost his match in front of Violet.

"I was worried that you got hurt," whispered Violet.

"I'm fine," Connor whispered back to her. He wondered if Violet had had an intrusive thought during his match. She sometimes imagined bad things happening to her friends because of her obsessive-compulsive disorder. "Nothing's broken, or even bruised," he added.

Violet was in the Infinity Rainbow Club with Connor. It was an after-school club for kids who had brain differences like Connor, Violet, and Luke. On the days they didn't have Taekwondo, they stayed after school to meet with the club.

After the red belts and the blue belts sparred, it was Luke's turn. He had a yellow belt with a green stripe like his partner. Luke had a close match but ended up winning. Connor was happy for him. Luke didn't freeze up like he had. Once the yellow belts sparred, it was time to move on to the next part of practice. Violet and the other white belts hadn't learned enough Taekwondo to fight in a match yet.

For the rest of practice, Connor had sparring drills. He went through the motions doing combinations of punches, kicks, and blocks. But he wasn't into it like he usually was. All he could think about was the hook kick that he took to the head.

"Jong yul!" yelled Master Park.

Everyone lined up by rank from right to left, forming lines from front to back. Haley was the highest rank at the front right corner of the dojang. The other pooms lined up to her left. Connor and Wyatt were on the far left of the front row. The rest of the color belts made three more rows. Violet was the lowest rank in the back row. Connor wished he didn't have to line up next to Wyatt. But rules were rules.

"Charyeot," said Master Park.

The class stood at attention with their arms straight by their sides.

"Kyeong-nye," she said.

They bowed.

"Ahnjoe," said Master Park.

Everyone sat on the floor in their spots. "I have an important announcement to make." She walked down the first line of students at the front of the class with her arms folded behind her back.

"We will be competing in the Three Rivers Taekwondo Tournament in two weeks. White belts will compete in poomsae, or forms. Color and junior black belts will compete in both poomsae and sparring."

Eyes opened wide. Mouths broke into smiles. Bodies shook in excitement. Everyone quietly celebrated in their spots. Even Connor.

Master Park walked down the second row of students and continued, "As you know, the belt tests are next week. If you pass your belt test, you will compete at your new rank."

Connor moved his hands along his well-worn red belt. Near the end, he found the edges of the black tape wrapped around the two tips of the belt.

If Connor passed his belt test, he would be a poom! He had always watched the junior black belt matches at his tournaments. His dream was to be one of them. Connor had watched other kids in his class advance through the belt ranks to become poom. And now it was his turn.

But Connor had a lot of training to do before the belt test. Poomsae. Self-defense techniques. Board breaks. Sparring. He would be tested on all the Taekwondo he had learned for the past six years. And over a hundred Korean words he had studied too. Connor needed to get back his focus, and fast. Wyatt had defeated Connor this time. But Connor wasn't going to let him win again.

CHAPTER 3

On Sunday morning, Connor woke up to Ace licking his hand. Connor rolled over in bed to look at the alarm clock on the nightstand. "It's too early, Ace. Go back to sleep."

Connor closed his eyes and started to drift off to sleep again. Ace barked. Not too loud. Just loud enough that Connor could hear him. But Connor didn't want to move. His muscles were *so* sore from Taekwondo practice yesterday.

Ace barked again. A little louder this time. Loud enough to let Connor know that Ace wasn't going back to sleep. But not loud enough to wake up Luke. Mom had said she would be up early shoveling snow. *Snow!* thought Connor. *That's a good reason to get out of bed.*

"Okay, you win," said Connor. "I'll take you outside."

Ace jumped up and down when Connor said "outside." His long pink tongue hung low from his mouth. Ace always panted when he was excited.

Connor stretched his body long and wide across his bed and then climbed out.

Ace had a pair of black sweatpants in his mouth.

"Are those clean or dirty?" Connor put out his hand.

Ace dropped the pants in Connor's hand and sniffed. Connor smelled them too. "Definitely dirty."

Connor tossed the sweatpants in his laundry hamper. At his window, he lifted one of the blinds and peeked out at the backyard. A thick white blanket of snow covered the grass.

"We got snow, Ace!" Connor jumped up and down. Ace did too.

Connor found a pile of clothes in the corner of his room. Clean clothes that Mom had told him to put away yesterday. He had meant to put them away. But Connor had *so many* superhero sweatpants, shirts, underwear, and socks to put away.

Connor had been running late for Taekwondo practice too. He didn't want to do twenty-five push-ups for being late. Then when Connor had gotten back from practice, he was too tired to put away laundry. So he had decided the clothes could wait until morning. But now Ace was waiting to go outside. And putting away laundry couldn't beat playing in the snow. *I'll do it after breakfast*, thought Connor.

Ace pulled a pair of gray sweatpants and a black T-shirt with a big green superhero out of the pile. Connor wasn't sure if dogs could have ADHD. But even if Ace did, Connor knew Ace was more focused than he was. *What would I do without Ace?* thought Connor.

"Thanks, Ace." Connor gave him a big hug. He rested his head on Ace's back. "Too bad you can't fold clothes too."

Ace barked. Maybe they would put that pile of clothes away when they came back inside. Doing laundry didn't seem so hard with Ace to help. And having Ace to talk to made everything easier.

Mom was on the front porch shoveling snow. Sometimes Connor helped her. But not today. He knew

Mom liked the exercise. And Connor liked walking with Ace better.

Connor opened the front door to let Mom know he would be in the backyard with Ace. When Connor opened the back door, Ace ran across the porch and into the fenced-in yard. Connor chased after him. Circling around the yard, Ace stamped his pawprints. He stopped in the middle of the yard to lick snow from the ground. With his white nose, Ace looked up at Connor.

Connor grabbed a handful of snow and shivered. That was when he realized he didn't have gloves on. Or a hat. Or even a winter coat. Mom wouldn't be happy about that. She wouldn't yell. But Mom would make him go back inside to get it.

And she would explain for the hundredth time why Connor had to wear a winter coat. He knew why he needed to wear it. And Connor knew that Ace had a double coat of fur without even trying. But Connor couldn't always remember to put on his coat.

He went back inside to get it. But Connor couldn't find his coat in the closet. That was where he was supposed to keep it. But Connor didn't always remember to put it away either.

He raced around the house until he spotted his coat on a chair in the kitchen. Connor put it on and roamed around the house again, looking for his beanie and gloves. One glove was on the kitchen floor. He must have dropped it there yesterday. And the other glove was tossed on the couch in the living room with his beanie. Connor had no idea how those got there.

When he was ready to go back outside, Connor realized that he had forgotten to shut the back door when he came in. *Great*, he thought. *I let all the cold air in again.* Mom would say Connor needed to slow down and focus. And Mom would be right. *Why can't I focus?* he wondered.

While Connor was gone, Ace had made hundreds of pawprints in the snow. Now Ace stood in the middle of the yard waiting for Connor to come out. They walked on the snow-covered path through the wooded part of the backyard. The same path they walked on every morning no matter how cold it was outside.

The sun flickered through the tall trees full of snow-covered pine needles. The blue jays whistled and flapped their wings.

"I lost a sparring match yesterday," Connor said. "It was against Wyatt."

Ace looked at Connor and tilted his head to the side. Connor took that as a sign that Ace was listening.

"You remember him, right?" asked Connor. "My biggest rival on the Titans. My archenemy. I froze up during the match. And he landed nakka-chagi—a hook kick—on my head to win. Can you believe it?"

Ace sniffed a bush and lifted his leg to water it. The white snow on the bush melted into a yellow pile on the ground.

Connor laughed. "Yeah, that's how I feel about Wyatt too."

Connor didn't want to tell Mom what had happened at Taekwondo. And he wouldn't see Dad until he stayed at his house next weekend. Sometimes Connor just needed someone to listen. Not to talk back. And Ace was always there when he needed him. Like when Dad left after the divorce. Connor could talk to Ace about anything.

Dad was a veterinarian—a doctor for animals. He had taught Connor how to take good care of Ace. Like how to brush Ace's teeth and double coat. And how much food to feed him.

Being outside on his walks with Ace always made Connor feel lighter. Like a weight had been lifted off of him. He felt free to move in a way that he never felt indoors.

Connor and Ace came back out of the woods. Ace found a snowdrift. It was twice as deep as the snow in the rest of the yard. Ace rolled onto his back and kicked his feet into the air. Snow flew off his paws, sprinkling onto the ground around him.

Connor took in a deep breath of cold air and let it out slowly. He could breathe easier outside. Playing in the snow with Ace was just what he needed to calm his body and mind.

CHAPTER 4

After breakfast, Connor *finally* put away his clothes. Mom wouldn't let Connor practice Taekwondo until he cleaned up his room.

Connor *hated* cleaning up. But he liked having a clean bedroom. Being able to walk around without tripping over his superhero books and action figures was a big improvement. And Ace had more space around his dog bed too.

Connor changed into his dobok and knotted his belt around his waist. Ace raced downstairs in front of Connor. And when Connor got to the first floor, he opened the door to another flight of stairs. Ace raced down those too.

In the basement, Luke had his back to Connor. But Connor could see Luke's reflection in the large mirror across the front of the room. Luke stood in *junbi*, or ready stance, with his arms slightly bent. His fists were just below his yellow belt with green stripe.

The dojang in the basement looked a lot like Master Park's. But the basement was smaller. The interlocking blue foam squares made one sparring ring in the middle. Red foam squares covered the rest of the floor.

Luke turned to the left and executed a low block, using his forearm. Then he did a high front kick, with the ball of his foot aimed for the head of an imaginary opponent, followed by a double punch. Luke turned to his right, repeating these moves on the other side.

Luke paused in a walking stance with a knife hand strike at the neck of his imaginary opponent. "What comes after this part?" He stayed frozen in position.

Connor didn't respond.

"Are you even watching?" Luke turned toward Connor.

"Watching what?" Connor scratched Ace's belly while Ace rolled around on his back.

"My Taegeuk Sam Jang form," said Luke. It was Luke's poomsae for his green belt test.

"I saw some of it." Connor stood up and bowed before stepping onto the foam-padded floor. Master Park said that bowing when entering and leaving a dojang showed respect for the training room. And Mom wanted Connor and Luke to carry out the same Taekwondo tradition in their home dojang.

Luke stomped across the floor to Connor. "I forget what comes next. I know my form. I do it all the time in class. But I need to do it by myself for the test. And I can't." Luke spun around in circles. He put the palms of his hands on his forehead, covering his face with his arms.

Connor paced back and forth. His mind raced through all the forms he needed to know. Connor had to know his new poomsae *Koryeo*. But he also had to know eight other Taegeuk forms he had learned along the way like Taegeuk Sam Jang. And then there were the kicks and hand strikes for the board breaks. The self-defense techniques. Not to mention all the new Korean words on his flashcards. Connor's head felt like it was spinning.

"I don't have time to help you. I have to get ready for *my* belt test. Junior black belt is a big deal. You're going to have to practice on your own this time."

Tears formed in Luke's eyes. And his eyebrows furrowed. "I keep messing up. I don't know what to do."

Ace carried a padded kicking target between Connor and Luke, as if Ace knew they weren't getting along and the kicking target was his way of trying to bring them back together. Luke had a half-smile on his face. He ran his hand along Ace's back to pet him.

Connor bowed to Ace and took the paddle from his mouth. Connor smacked the two sides of the clamshell kicking target together. Ace jumped up and down at the loud clapping noise that it made. "Thanks, Ace," Connor said.

Connor moved to a back corner of the room and put the kicking target down.

Koryeo started with Connor's favorite Taekwondo stance. *Tongmilgi-junbi*. Master Park also called it the log-pushing posture. Connor breathed in deep and imagined that he was pulling a log toward his chest. Then he breathed out, using the outside edges of his curved hands to push the imaginary log out slowly. Tongmilgi-junbi always made Connor feel strong with his muscles and relaxed in his mind.

The biggest challenge for Connor was remembering all the moves for his poomsae. Before practicing Koryeo with power, he ran through all the movements without putting any force into them. Connor could see the sequence for his form playing in his head like a video. Moving his arms and legs gently, Connor looked like a puppet.

He made it all the way through the form without forgetting what came next. Connor was so proud of himself. But he didn't feel so great when he looked over at Luke. Luke started and stopped Taegeuk Sam Jang. And started and stopped it again. Luke was pretty much stuck in the same spot that he was in when Connor had first watched him.

It wouldn't have taken that long for Connor to show Luke how to do the next moves in his form. Probably only a few minutes. And it would've saved Luke from getting so upset for forgetting. This time Connor was a bad big brother. And he knew it.

Mom appeared in the mirror of the home dojang. She was behind Connor at the bottom of the basement stairs. Facing the front of the dojang, she bowed before entering. Mom wore her black belt dobok. It looked the same as Connor and Luke's color belt uniform, but it had black trim around the v-shaped neckline like Master Park's.

Mom's black belt had her name embroidered on it. And at the tip of the belt, one gold bar showed that she was a first-degree black belt.

Mom used to compete in Taekwondo tournaments when she was in college. She was the reason Connor and Luke first got involved in martial arts. She didn't learn Taekwondo until she was an adult. But she knew that martial arts training would help Connor and Luke focus better, so she had started them early.

Connor and Luke almost always practiced on weekends with Mom. It was one of their favorite things to do together. And Ace was like a mascot cheering them on.

But Connor missed having Dad there too. For the first year after the divorce, Connor had wished Dad would surprise them in the dojang. That he would show up in his tracksuit like he used to. Dad didn't have a dobok or any official Taekwondo training.

But after three years, Connor wasn't expecting Dad to show up in the dojang anymore.

"How's it going?" Mom asked.

"Connor wouldn't help me with Taegeuk Sam Jang." Luke frowned.

Mom turned to Connor. "Is that true?"

Connor lowered his head. "Yes, but I have to get ready for *my* belt test." He knew he didn't have a good excuse before he even finished giving one.

Mom gave Connor the look she always gave him when she disapproved. Her lips tight together. Her piercing stare. And her arms crossed. Mom didn't have to say a word. Connor knew she was upset that he didn't help Luke. And he wasn't happy with himself either for letting Luke down.

"I'm really sorry, Luke." Connor put his arm around Luke's shoulder. "I should've helped you with your form."

Mom pointed to the floor. "Ahnjoe."

Connor and Luke sat down. Ace plopped down next to Connor and rested his head in Connor's lap. Mom joined them on the floor.

"I'm so proud of both of you for coming this far in Taekwondo," said Mom. "You've been working hard for months to learn everything for your belt tests. But we have to stick together as a family. And that means helping each other." She looked at Connor. "Teaching other people Taekwondo is part of being a black belt."

"Yes, Ma'am . . . Mom," said Connor.

Mom laughed. Connor and Luke did too. To show respect, female black belts were called Ma'am. Connor and Luke and the rest of their Taekwondo class called Master Park and Haley Ma'am. But Connor always had trouble deciding what to call Mom in their dojang.

Connor and Mom worked with Luke until he made it all the way through Taegeuk Sam Jang on his own without getting stuck.

"Way to go, Luke," said Connor.

Connor performed Koryeo for Mom and Luke. This time he didn't hold back. He put all his energy into every one of his moves. He felt strong and powerful.

Connor and Luke worked on their poomsae from earlier belt tests too. Mom went back and forth between them in case they needed help.

"Let's take a break from forms," said Mom. "Ace"— she pointed to the clamshell paddle—"bring me a kicking target."

Ace picked it up with his mouth and dropped it in Mom's hand.

"Good boy." Mom petted Ace on the head. "Let's review Newton's First Law of Motion."

"An object at rest stays at rest," said Luke.

Mom held the kicking target still.

"Unless acted upon by an outside force," said Connor.

Mom smacked one side of the clamshell target with her hand, making a loud clapping noise. She was a professor who taught physics to college students. She loved to talk about what she called the science of Taekwondo.

Mom handed the kicking paddle to Connor. "Hold it for dollyeo-chagi."

Connor got into a front stance. His front leg was bent and his back leg straight like he was standing in a big lunge. He held the clamshell paddle tightly on the handle with both hands out in front of his chest. He knew Mom's roundhouse kicks were powerful. He needed a strong base to hold the target for her.

Mom stood facing Connor in a fighting stance, ready to strike the target. "When you chamber your leg for dollyeo-chagi"—Mom lifted her right leg and pointed her knee at the target. She pivoted on her left foot— "potential energy is temporarily stored in the muscles of your leg and foot." Mom returned to fighting stance.

"Potential energy becomes kinetic energy when you kick a target or an opponent," continued Mom. "Kinetic energy is the energy of motion." She threw a roundhouse kick. "USS!"

Boom!

It sounded like thunder when the top of Mom's foot hit the target. "Speed can make your kick more powerful. And the size of the person kicking matters too." She took the paddle from Connor and held it for him to practice dollyeo-chagi.

Then she held the target for Luke to work on his roundhouse kicks too. Ace jumped up and down like he was dancing to the rhythm of the loud clapping noises.

Connor and Luke even practiced their board breaks. Not with wooden boards like the ones Master Park used for belt tests. At home, they had reusable plastic boards. The interlocking plastic only came apart if they had enough power in their hand strikes and kicks. And then they would put the plastic pieces together and use it again.

Ace gave Luke his green plastic board. Mom held it while Luke worked on nakka-chagi. Connor couldn't watch. It reminded him of the hook kick Wyatt had landed on his head. Ace gave Connor his two boards— red and black. The black board was especially hard to break. But it was the board he would be using more when he became a poom.

Mom held the black board and Luke the red board for Connor's *narae-chagi.* Ace always barked the loudest for his double kicks. Then Mom and Luke each held one side of the black board for Connor's *yeop-chagi.* His side kick broke the plastic board into two pieces with the outside edge of his foot.

Connor still had a lot of practicing to do before his junior black belt test. But having his family—and even Ace—to help him prepare made him feel ready to take on the challenge.

CHAPTER 5

Connor was really looking forward to the first day of school after winter break. It had been twelve days since he had seen his friends, except for Violet. But he couldn't have expected the big change in his classroom on Monday morning.

Wyatt.

It was bad enough that he would be coming to Master Park's dojang three times a week. But now he was in Mr. Frost's fourth-grade class too. Wyatt must have moved into a house close to Connor. Connor didn't know of any houses for sale in his neighborhood. But he decided that if Wyatt turned out to be a new neighbor, he would ask Mom if they could move.

After morning routines and independent reading, Connor had teacher time with his friends Jasmine and Molly. Their special education teacher, Ms. Daisy, sat at a table near a window in the back of the classroom. She was also in charge of the Infinity Rainbow Club after school.

Ms. Daisy wore a black dress covered in math problems and tall black boots. The problems on Ms. Daisy's dress looked like they were handwritten on a blackboard. Addition. Subtraction. Multiplication. And division. Connor didn't know how to solve the other math problems on her dress. The mix of letters, numbers, and signs scared him.

But Connor liked when Ms. Daisy wore the math dress. Not because math was his favorite subject. Far from it. But he loved how the pattern on her dress was confusing and disorganized. Like Ms. Daisy's dress, Connor's brain had geometric shapes, fractions, and formulas that floated around it. He had trouble focusing on just one calculation at a time.

Connor plopped down in a seat across from Ms. Daisy at the table. From there, he had the best view of the snow falling outside the window. He had spotted blue jays, cardinals, deer, squirrels, and chipmunks from this seat before. No wildlife was out in the snow now. But he could see what looked like deer tracks.

In another fourth-grade classroom, his best friend, Nick, had spotted a turkey a few months ago. Connor wished he could be with Nick now, catching snowflakes on his tongue outside. It would sure beat solving math word problems.

Jasmine sat on one side of Connor and Molly on the other. And Wyatt took the chair across from him. Connor looked at Ms. Daisy, waiting for her to tell Wyatt that he was at the wrong table. But Ms. Daisy didn't say anything. *Does she see Wyatt?* wondered Connor.

Ms. Daisy handed all of them a stapled packet of math word problems. She gave Wyatt a few pieces of graph paper too. Ms. Daisy welcomed Wyatt to the school and told him about the Infinity Rainbow Club.

Connor was confused. The only kids who had teacher time with Ms. Daisy and belonged to the club had different brains like him.

Jasmine was in the club. She was autistic like Nick. For her, autism meant using her tablet to communicate, doing things the same way every time, and flapping her hands when she got excited.

Molly could be in the club, but she wasn't. She helped at her family bakery after school instead. Molly had dyspraxia. She had trouble with handwriting, focusing on directions, and balancing on the balls in the sensory gym. *But Wyatt doesn't have a different brain like us*, thought Connor. *Does he?*

Connor put his name on the packet and flipped through the pages. One word problem on each page. Five word problems total. Ms. Daisy called this chunking. Having only one word problem to solve at a time was supposed to make it easier to focus.

"We'll work on the first word problem together," said Ms. Daisy. "Let's read the text one piece at a time. We're going to pause when we get to a number and draw each step of the problem. Molly, please read the first line."

"Emma went to a bakery to buy sweets," said Molly.

"Okay, nothing to draw yet," said Ms. Daisy. "Go ahead to the next part, Molly."

"She bought one heart-shaped cake for six dollars and fifty-nine cents," said Molly.

"Stop," said Ms. Daisy. "What would you draw with that information?"

"A heart," said Molly. "With six dollars and fifty-nine cents inside of it." Holding the squishy purple grip on her pencil, she drew the heart. Molly held her packet up for the group.

"Great idea!" said Ms. Daisy.

Everyone drew a heart like Molly's at the top of their paper. Except for Wyatt. He used his graph paper instead.

This is going to take forever, thought Connor.

"Connor, please read the next item," said Ms. Daisy.

"Two star-shaped cupcakes for two dollars and fourteen cents each," said Connor. "I would draw two stars with two dollars and fourteen cents inside each one." He didn't want to draw anything. *What a waste of time!* But he drew the stars under the heart like Ms. Daisy wanted him to. And he showed the group his work. Connor knew he couldn't get in trouble if he followed the directions.

$2.14 + $2.14 = $4.28

"Great," said Ms. Daisy. "Jasmine, the next line, please."

Connor took his fidget spinner out of his pocket and gave it a spin.

Jasmine played the next part of the word problem on her tablet. She used it to read out loud for her because she didn't speak. Connor thought that Jasmine always had cool ideas. Like her idea to add long jump as an event for the recess Snow Games.

The voice on Jasmine's tablet said, "Two triangle-shaped cookies for one dollar and eight cents each." With her smart pen, Jasmine drew two triangles on her tablet with $1.08 inside each of them. Jasmine held up her tablet to show the group:

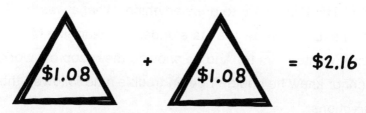

"Excellent, Jasmine!" said Ms. Daisy. "Wyatt, could you finish reading the word problem?"

"Emma started with fifteen dollars," said Wyatt. "How much money does she have left?" He tapped his pencil on the table. And his knee moved up and down in rhythm with the tapping. "So we need to figure out how much money Emma spent first."

"Right," said Ms. Daisy. "How can you calculate that number?"

"By adding the cost for the cake, cupcakes, and cookies," Wyatt said.

Show-off, thought Connor.

On his graph paper, Wyatt added up the amount for each type of sweet. He showed the group what he had drawn. The numbers were lined up neatly in boxes on the graph paper.

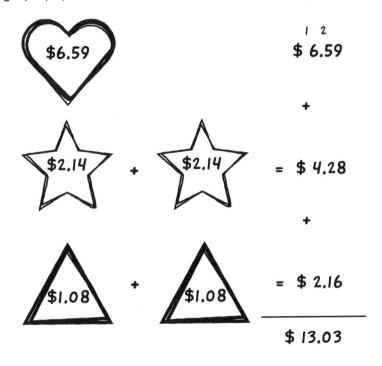

$$
\begin{array}{r}
{}^{1\ 2} \\
\$\ 6.59 \\
+ \\
=\ \$\ 4.28 \\
+ \\
=\ \$\ 2.16 \\
\hline
\$\ 13.03
\end{array}
$$

"Very good," said Ms. Daisy. "Molly, how do we find out how much money Emma had left?"

"Subtract thirteen dollars and three cents from fifteen dollars." Molly subtracted the numbers on her paper. "The answer is one dollar and ninety-seven cents." She shared her work with the group.

$$
\begin{array}{r}
\overset{4\ \ 9\ \ 1}{\$\ 15.\ 00} \\
-\ 13.\ 03 \\
\hline
\$\ \ \ \ 1.97
\end{array}
$$

"Great job!" said Ms. Daisy. "Try the next word problem on your own. Make sure you draw a *visual* for each step of the word problem. This will help you break it down into smaller chunks."

But Connor wasn't convinced that chunking would help. Especially if he had to do the word problem on his own. He still had to *solve* the whole problem, even if it was only one step at a time. He flipped his packet to the next page. Just looking at the words and numbers in the problem was enough to make his brain flood with information. Like the calculations swimming all over Ms. Daisy's dress.

CHAPTER 6

Connor stared at the word problem until he couldn't see the letters and numbers on the page anymore. His brain took in every sound that could be heard at his table. Jasmine flapped her hands. Molly played with her long black braid. Wyatt fidgeted in his seat. Ms. Daisy rustled papers. Not to mention the noise from the other kids behind Connor. It wasn't that he couldn't focus. But that he focused on everything at the same time. And he couldn't stop his brain from hearing all the noises.

The only thing that helped sometimes was his noise-canceling headphones. Connor pulled them out of his backpack and put them on.

Connor read the whole paragraph to himself.

Brian goes shopping for school supplies. He buys a box of crayons for $2.29, a notebook for $1.34, two folders for $1.10 each, and two pencils for 50 cents each. If he has $10, how much money will he have left?

Ms. Daisy had said not to read it all at once. But Connor didn't want to spend *all* day drawing school supplies with numbers inside them. *That would waste so much time!* Connor thought he could solve the problem a lot faster if he did it his way.

But the words and numbers blurred on the page. He forgot what he was reading as he was reading it. And by the time Connor finished reading the last line of the problem, he couldn't remember any of it.

Ms. Daisy tapped him on the shoulder. Connor hadn't even written anything on his paper yet. *How does she know I'm not doing it her way?* Ms. Daisy pointed to his chair. Connor was hanging on the edge of it. And he had no idea that he was about to fall.

Connor had slid off his chair in class more than a few times. Now *that* was embarrassing. He even had a scar on his leg from when he fell off a big chair at home. Connor moved back to the center of his seat. Ms. Daisy stepped away to check on the rest of the group.

I need to add, thought Connor. *No, subtract.* He scanned the numbers in the word problem again. *Wait. Wait. I got it. I need to add and then subtract.*

Wyatt shook his hand like he was writing so fast he had a cramp in it. Connor decided that he wouldn't look over at Wyatt anymore. If he pretended that Wyatt wasn't there, he would be able to focus better. But Connor was trying so hard to ignore Wyatt that it made him think about Wyatt even more.

Connor had to hurry up and finish the word problem. He was determined to get it done before Wyatt. He *had* to. Connor hated word problems. But he sure wasn't going to let Wyatt beat him in math class. Connor wrote the first four numbers on his paper as fast as he could. Connor added them together. Then, he subtracted them from ten.

"Four dollars and seventy-seven cents!" Connor blurted out. He didn't mean to shout out the answer. The number just came spilling out of his mouth before he could stop it. Mom called it impulsive behavior when he said or did something without thinking first.

Jasmine and Molly looked at him. But they turned away quickly. They were used to him blurting out answers and didn't make a big deal about it. But Wyatt and a few other kids at tables next to them stared at Connor. Like they thought something was wrong with him. He could feel his face getting red. And redder.

Connor knew Jasmine was still using her smart pen to draw the steps of the problem on her tablet. And Molly and Wyatt were still solving the problem on their papers. But Connor *really* wanted to be the first one done. And he wanted everyone to know he was the first one done too. But not like this.

"Connor, remember what we talked about when working in groups," said Ms. Daisy. "You need to wait quietly for everyone to finish. Please don't say the answer out loud until I call on you." Connor knew he was supposed to wait. Ms. Daisy only reminded him every day. Waiting was hard when it was just Jasmine and Molly. But waiting for an archenemy to finish was impossible.

"I know," said Connor. "I'm sorry." He kept replaying a video in his head of what had just happened. *This isn't going to be an easy day*, thought Connor. *I can't do anything right*.

"Connor, you didn't get the answer correct," said Ms. Daisy. "Please go back and try solving the problem again. But this time, slow down on each step. And draw the pictures like you did for the first problem."

What! thought Connor. *This is unbelievable*. It was bad enough that he embarrassed himself in front of the whole group. Maybe even the whole class. But he didn't even do the problem the right way.

Connor took a deep breath in and out. If he could break a board in Taekwondo, he could solve a word problem in math class. *Perseverance*, thought Connor. *To not give up even when it is hard to keep going*.

"Okay, I'll draw the pictures." Connor read the first part of the problem again until he got to a number. On his paper, he drew a box of crayons, a notebook, two folders, and two pencils. Connor put the cost of each item in the drawings too. He knew then that he had made two big mistakes. He didn't have the cost of *two* folders and *two* pencils when he solved the problem the first time.

Connor continued to work on the math problem exactly the way Ms. Daisy had shown him. It was just like learning the pattern of moves for a poomsae. When he finished his work, Connor looked around the table. He was the last one done. But no one said anything about it. Or looked at him funny. Not even Wyatt.

Maybe Ms. Daisy is right, thought Connor. *Chunking does make the word problem easier.* He was able to follow along when the group worked on the first problem together. It took *forever*. But the answer was right. And

Connor thought that he got the second word problem right this time too. Even if he didn't, Connor knew that he gave it his best shot. He stayed focused for an entire word problem. On his own. For the first time ever. And that was something.

CHAPTER 7

For recess, Connor put on his snow gear. A winter coat, snow pants, boots, gloves, and a hat.

Why can't the whole school day be outside? wondered Connor. He could draw word problems in the snow. Read in an igloo. Build a snowman for art. And race through a snow-covered obstacle course for gym.

Connor fist-bumped Nick and Ruby on the playground. The last time Connor had seen them was before winter break. Jasmine, Violet, and Molly joined them too.

Nick flapped his hands. "Welcome to the Snow Games!"

Jasmine flapped her hands too. She had a strong grip on her tablet that waved around in the air. She took it almost everywhere. Even in the snow. She had a thick waterproof case on her tablet to protect it from getting wet.

Connor and Violet jumped up and down and spun in circles. And Ruby and Molly jumped up and down too.

They all had their own way of showing their excitement for the Snow Games. And Connor never felt silly spinning in circles around his friends.

The Snow Games were a tradition that Connor and Nick had started last school year. Now every time they had recess in the snow, they continued the tradition.

The first event was the long jump. Violet drew a starting line in the snow with her boot. Molly ran up to the line and jumped. She landed on her feet. But she was a little off balance. She swayed back and forth, fighting to stay on her feet. And she did it. The back of her footprint would mark the length of her jump.

"How's Taekwondo?" Nick asked Connor.

Connor had been waiting to tell Nick what happened at practice on Saturday. Connor didn't keep anything from his best friend.

"I lost a sparring match to Wyatt," said Connor.

Ruby jumped next. When she launched herself in the air, her red hair poked out of her ice hockey beanie. Her jump was longer than Molly's. The distance between them was about the length of a notebook.

"Your rival from the Titans?" Nick asked Connor. "I thought you only fought him at tournaments."

"Wyatt *used to be* on the Titans," said Connor. "But now he's at Master Park's dojang."

"No way!" said Nick. "Haley said a new kid joined the Lions. And that he was good. But she didn't say it was *Wyatt*."

Jasmine did a practice run up to the line to measure her steps before jumping. She was serious about the long jump. Swinging her hands and feet midair, Jasmine landed in front of Ruby's footprint. Ace would probably fit in the gap if he were lying down in the snow between Ruby's and Jasmine's footprints. It was a tough length to beat.

"And even worse," said Connor to Nick. "Wyatt just started school here today too. And he's in my class."

"You're kidding," said Nick.

"I wish I were." Connor sighed.

"Where is he?" Nick looked around the field. "Indoor recess?"

"No." Connor pointed to the other side of the field. "Over there."

Wyatt was talking to Mr. Frost. Connor could pick out Mr. Frost from anywhere with his monster hat. The green beanie with one big eyeball on the front. And different-colored eyeballs poking out from the hat in all directions.

Mr. Frost wore anything. That was what Connor liked most about him.

Connor was pretty sure Mr. Frost was telling Wyatt the long list of outdoor recess rules.

Violet jumped next. She made it further than Molly's footprint. But not quite as far as Ruby's. Violet was in third place.

"You're up, Connor," said Violet.

Connor was in the lead after his jump. But then Nick passed him up. Nick ended up in first place. And Connor took second. The long jump was always Nick's best event.

The next event was the obstacle course on the playground. Nick, Ruby, and Molly set up snow piles to hurdle over. Connor, Violet, and Jasmine created a maze through the snow. In the corner of the playground, they dug through the snow to uncover their secret stash of sticks. Violet counted the small branches into piles of seven. The sticks would mark the path to zigzag through the maze.

"You told me to tell you when you're being compulsive," Connor said to Violet. "I know you're counting the sticks over and over to put them in piles of seven."

Violet nodded. Connor knew the reminders from her friends helped Violet with her OCD. After they talked, Connor and Violet worked with Jasmine to lay out the sticks without counting them.

Wyatt wandered over to the playground. He was alone. Connor ignored him, hoping he would just leave eventually.

"Hey, Wyatt," said Molly. "Do you want to join us? We're doing what we call the Snow Games. We're just about to start an obstacle course."

Uh-oh, thought Connor.

"Sure, sounds fun," said Wyatt.

Molly introduced Wyatt to Nick, Violet, and Ruby. Wyatt already knew Jasmine from Mr. Frost's class. And of course, Wyatt had a long history with Connor.

Connor was having so much fun with his friends until Wyatt showed up. *Why did Molly have to go and ruin it for me?* thought Connor. *Could my day get any worse?*

The obstacle course only had enough room for two kids to compete at the same time. The winners of each race would move on to the next round. Molly was always a referee for the obstacle course. She didn't want to risk getting hurt in a race. Balance was really hard for her, especially in the snow with boots.

In the first round, Connor was paired up with Nick. Jasmine with Ruby. And Violet with Wyatt. They raced through the snow maze. Molly used her watch to time the races.

Connor, Jasmine, and Wyatt won and moved on to the next round. But since Wyatt had the fastest time, he got to skip a round. Connor raced Jasmine in the second round. And after he won, Connor was set to compete against Wyatt in the final round.

Connor lined up next to Wyatt. The obstacle course was Connor's event. *He* was the reigning champion. And Connor was sure that Wyatt wasn't going to beat him at his event.

In the maze, Connor could see Wyatt gaining on him from the corner of his eye. Connor sped up. Then Wyatt sped up. They were neck and neck. Wyatt tried to pass Connor. But Connor tripped and fell forward. With the twists and turns of the path, Connor ended up falling into a pile of snow. He used his forearms to break his fall but still sank down in the snow. His face ended up in it too.

Connor decided that he couldn't have tripped on his own. It must have been Wyatt's fault. Connor pushed himself halfway up and looked toward Mr. Frost. He was

on the far side of the field facing the other direction. *Of course, he didn't see Wyatt trip me*, thought Connor. *And Wyatt did it on purpose.*

Wyatt turned his head and looked behind him. He didn't continue the race. Wyatt ran back toward Connor instead. Wyatt reached out his hand. Connor didn't take it. *Like I would fall for that*, thought Connor. *It's bad enough that Wyatt face-planted me in the snow.*

Connor was *so* angry. He finally stood up and got into a fighting stance. Connor bounced on his boots in front of Wyatt with his gloved fists up in the air. Sparring in snow gear wouldn't be easy. But Connor was ready for a rematch.

"What are you doing?" Wyatt laughed, making Connor even more angry. "I'm not fighting you here."

"Why not?" Connor asked, even though he knew it would be wrong to use his Taekwondo to fight outside the dojang. Master Park said martial arts outside of practice and tournaments should only be used to defend, not to strike first. But he had to prove to himself that he was *not* a loser.

"I only fight in the dojang," said Wyatt.

"You're not a Lion!" As soon as he blurted it out, Connor knew that he shouldn't have. He was too loud *and* mean. But sometimes Connor said words out loud that he didn't mean to say. His impulsive behavior was out of his control. Connor stood there frozen in a fighting stance.

Nick ran over to Connor and lowered Connor's fists. "Not here."

Connor knew he should apologize, but he couldn't get the words out before Wyatt started to walk away from the playground.

Connor turned around. Violet, Jasmine, Ruby, and Molly were all staring at him. And a few other fourth graders nearby were staring at him too.

"Why do you have such a problem with Wyatt anyway?" asked Violet. "He seems nice."

"He *seems* nice," said Connor. "He's not."

"What did he do to you besides win a sparring match against you?" said Violet.

"He tripped me," said Connor. "Didn't you see?"

"He didn't trip you," said Violet. "You fell."

"You just don't get it," said Connor. "I've been fighting Wyatt in Taekwondo tournaments since I was five."

"So what?" said Violet.

"He was on the Titans. Our biggest rival," said Connor. "You haven't been to a tournament yet. Nick understands what it's like. Don't you?"

"I've seen your tournaments," said Nick. "And I know Wyatt is your rival. But I don't understand why you got so mad at Wyatt today. I mean, he didn't finish the obstacle course because he saw you fall. He tried to help you up too."

"*You* don't understand," Connor said. "It's a Taekwondo thing." He knew he was being mean to Nick. But Connor couldn't stop himself. All the anger he had built up inside came spilling out. "And you don't know anything about Taekwondo."

Connor was always competing with Wyatt. Sparring in Taekwondo. Solving word problems in math class. And racing in an obstacle course at recess. Connor wanted to win so badly that all he could think about was winning. And now he was fighting with his best friend. All because of Wyatt. *Why can't he just leave me alone?* thought Connor.

Mr. Frost jogged toward Connor and his friends and blew his whistle. "Time to go back inside!"

All the fourth graders groaned. Connor too. He let his friends go in front of him back to the school. Connor didn't want to talk to any of them. He needed some time alone. Connor stomped through the snow slowly toward the school by himself. But Mr. Frost blew his whistle again to hurry everyone along.

Connor took off his winter coat in the crowded hallway. He couldn't avoid making eye contact with Wyatt. Their eyes met for only a moment before Connor looked away. He worried that Wyatt would tell everyone in fourth grade that he froze up in Taekwondo class. That Connor couldn't block or punch or kick. That he couldn't fight in a real match. And then, everyone would laugh.

Pulling off his snow pants, he decided what he had to do. Connor was going to show Wyatt and everyone else that he was the better fighter. Even if Connor had to wait to fight Wyatt until they were in the dojang again.

CHAPTER 8

Connor had prepared for his junior black belt test all week long. Some days at Master Park's dojang and other days at home. Mom had quizzed Connor and Luke on Korean words every night. Connor had practiced his self-defense techniques with Luke over and over again. Connor had done Koryeo and the eight Taegeuk forms so many times that he dreamt about poomsae. He had fought sparring matches in his head when he couldn't get in a ring. And Connor had broken his reusable plastic boards at least fifty times in the last week too.

On Saturday, it was time for the big test. Dad took Connor and Luke to the dojang. With his Taekwondo bag slung over his shoulder, Connor put his arms at his sides and bowed at the entrance. Luke and Dad followed Connor into the dojang and bowed too.

Kids crowded the foam-padded floor. Some warmed up with stretches. Others practiced blocks, kicks, and punches in the air. And a few ran through their poomsae.

Connor and Luke put their bags full of sparring gear in the back of the room. Luke found the other kids who would be testing for their green belts. Connor warmed up on his own. He took a deep breath in and out. He jogged back and forth on the foam-padded floor, the balls of his feet sinking into it.

On one side of the room, chairs had been set up for spectators. Violet's parents, grandma, brother Bo, and Nick were already in seats. Dad took the seat next to Mom.

Connor used to think that if Mom and Dad sat next to each other at belt tests and tournaments, they might get back together. But they had sat next to each other for the past three years and nothing had changed. Connor was glad they still talked to each other. But sometimes he wanted more. Connor wanted them to smile at each other the way they smiled at him.

Nick held up a poster. It looked like a comic with figures doing Taekwondo. One drawing was a boy in a dobok wearing a half red and half black belt. The boy had launched himself in the air for a flying side kick. Another boy in a green belt had his foot up at head level for a hook kick. A girl in a yellow belt snapped a front kick. And another girl in a poom belt had her arm out between two fighters like she was the referee for a sparring match. At the top of the poster, it said, "Go Lions!" Connor gave Nick two thumbs up.

In the front of the room, a long table was covered with a white cloth. It was the table Master Park usually set up on belt test days. The judges would sit on the three chairs behind the table. Master Park always invited two other Master Black Belts from other dojangs to judge the belt tests with her. Haley and the other pooms assisted with the tests too.

The neatly folded color belts were stacked on the table. Yellow, green, blue, and red. Rolls of green, blue, red, and black tape for the stripes too. At the far end of the table sat a half-red and half-black poom belt. Connor had expected to see two of them there. He looked around the room, but he didn't see Wyatt. *Isn't he testing too?*

Connor found Violet in the middle of the dojang. She was practicing her poomsae.

"Good luck today," he said.

"You too," Violet said. "I'm *so* worried about my first belt test. What if I forget everything?" She paced back and forth on the red foam squares.

"You won't," said Connor. "Just try not to think too much about it. You know all the kicks, punches, and blocks. You've practiced your form so many times that you'll just know what to do. You'll be fine. Trust me."

Connor believed in the words he had just told Violet. But he was anxious too. *Really* anxious. Connor wished *he* didn't think so much about everything he needed to know for his test. His mind kept racing through all the poomsae, self-defense techniques, and board breaks he needed to know.

"Thanks," said Violet. "I feel a little better. I just wish I could practice my form more before the test starts." She sighed.

"Seven times?" Connor looked at Violet knowingly.

"Yeah, that's what I was thinking," said Violet. "But I know I don't need to practice my form seven times. It feels better to say that out loud."

"You got this," said Connor. "Have you seen Wyatt?"

"Why are *you* looking for Wyatt?" Violet asked. "Not trying to start a fight, are you?"

"I just want to know if he's testing today," said Connor. "I don't think he's here."

Violet pointed to the front corner of the dojang. "He's up there with the junior black belts."

Connor saw Wyatt standing next to Haley and the other pooms. *What's Wyatt doing with them?* wondered Connor.

"Good morning, family and friends," Master Park said to the spectators. "Thank you so much for coming to watch the belt tests. All the students testing today have worked so hard to get here. They trained three times a week for many months to prepare for their promotion tests. You're welcome to take photos and videos. But please stay off the foam squares during testing."

Master Park turned toward the students in uniforms. "Jong yul!"

Everyone ran to line up by rank. The junior black belts and Wyatt too.

"Charyeot," said Master Park.

Everyone stood at attention with their arms by their sides.

"Kyeong-nye," she said.

They bowed.

Master Park joined the two other Master Black Belts sitting at the judges' table.

Haley led the class in *Taegeuk Il Jang.* All the belts knew this beginner form. Belt tests always started with it as a demonstration for the Master Black Belts and the spectators.

When the form was finished, the class bowed and was dismissed. While they waited for their turn to test, Connor, Luke, Violet, and the rest of the students sat cross-legged on the floor in the back of the dojang. But Wyatt went to the front of the room with the pooms again.

Wyatt had been a red belt with a black stripe for a long time. Connor knew this from fighting him in tournaments. But Wyatt had just joined Master Park's dojang last week. So maybe Master Park had told Wyatt to wait to take his test. *But if he isn't testing, why is he here?* wondered Connor.

Connor looked at the five tenets of Taekwondo that hung on the wall. He had memorized them long ago. Connor's favorite one was perseverance. Mom said it was the tenet that described him most. *Perseverance,* thought Connor. *To not give up even when it is hard to keep going.* And that was exactly what he would have to do to earn his junior black belt today.

"Connor!" yelled Haley.

"Yes, Ma'am!" Connor yelled back. He stood up and turned to the back of the room to fix his uniform like Master Park had taught him. Connor turned back around and ran to his spot for testing.

Haley called the names of two other red belts in his class too. They lined up next to Connor. Haley told the two red belts to be partners for their self-defense technique. And she called Wyatt to be Connor's partner. That was when Connor knew that Wyatt was there to help with *his* test. *But can I trust Wyatt?* thought Connor. *What if he trips me again?*

Connor had no choice but to be Wyatt's partner. Wyatt grabbed Connor's wrist. Connor escaped the wrist grab. He landed two knife hand strikes close to Wyatt's neck. "Hi-YAH!" And Connor threw yeop-chagi up toward Wyatt's head, The side kick stopped right before hitting Wyatt in the face. "Hi-YAH!" Connor's self-defense moves showed good control like Master Park and Mom had taught him.

The beginning of the belt test couldn't have gone any smoother for Connor. And Wyatt didn't make him look bad either. Connor was *so* focused. He had never felt so sure of himself in a belt test before. And Connor got to show Wyatt that he could defend himself too.

Connor returned to his seat in the back of the room. He tried hard not to think about anything. To completely clear his mind. To stay focused on what was happening right in front of him.

Luke was paired up with another student testing for his green belt. His attacker moved with an attempt to punch him in the face. But Luke blocked it and punched toward his attacker's stomach and face. "KYO!" He looked strong. More powerful than all the students testing with him. All the hours Luke had spent working on his self-defense techniques in the home dojang were worth it.

And Violet didn't forget any of her self-defense techniques either. She escaped wrist grabs from both sides. Connor thought she was really good at Taekwondo for a beginner.

Next up was poomsae. Connor was really worried about his forms. They had always been his weakness for belt tests no matter how much he practiced. And now that he was testing for a junior black belt, he had *so* many poomsae to remember. Freezing up during any of them would be a disaster. But all he had to do was stay focused for eight Taegeuk forms and Koryeo. No pressure at all.

Connor lined up with two red belts to do the eight Taegeuk forms together. He had worked hard on all of them for months. Connor could practically do the forms in his sleep. The room was so quiet. He exhaled hard with each move, making his blocks, kicks, and punches more powerful. All he could hear was the snapping of his uniform. And he felt the blood rushing through his body. He didn't make any mistakes. *Whew!*

But now was the real test. Koryeo. The red belts were dismissed. They didn't need to know Koryeo yet. And Connor was the only one testing for poom. So he would have to do Koryeo on his own.

Connor got into tongmilgi-junbi. The log pushing posture. Pulling the imaginary log toward his chest and

pushing the log out again made him feel unstoppable.
Connor made it through the double knife hand blocks,
the double kicks, the front kicks, and the low knife hand
blocks without any problems. Connor made it all the way
to the *kihap* in the middle of Koryeo. The part where he
yelled, "Hi-YAH!" And then he froze.

Connor stood there for what seemed like forever. His
mind was blank. It was like he forgot that he was in the
middle of a form. And that he forgot that he was in the
middle of a belt test too. His junior black belt test.

"Paro." Master Park told Connor to return to ready stance. She waited until he was ready.

"Shijak!" she yelled.

Connor took a deep breath in and out. And he started Koryeo from the beginning. But Connor froze *again*. He didn't even get as far as he had the first time.

"Paro," said Master Park.

Connor waited for the next command. His arms bent in front of him. His fists in front of his belt. But he didn't get another command this time. The judges whispered to each other at the table. And he waited. And waited.

Sweat dripped down Connor's face. All the muscles in his body tightened. He couldn't believe that he had messed up Koryeo. His junior black belt form. Not once, but twice. *Now what?* thought Connor. He had never frozen up twice before in a belt test. *Did I fail?*

Koryeo was the form he was supposed to know best. And Connor *did* know it best. He wanted so badly to have another chance. Connor knew he could do it. He just needed to get back his focus. But would Connor have another chance? Or was it already too late?

CHAPTER 9

Master Park called Connor up to the judges' table.
He stood in front of three Master Black Belts. Connor
blinked back tears. He couldn't cry at his belt test.

"I know that you can do Koryeo," said Master Park.
"And with a lot of power. I've seen you perform Koryeo
many times. But you need to show me and the other
Master Black Belts here that you can do it for your test.
We're going to give you one more chance after the rest
of the belts are done with their forms. Please take a seat
with the rest of the class."

"Yes, Ma'am!" Connor ran to the back of the room.
He wouldn't even look over at Mom and Dad. Connor
didn't want to see them looking sorry for him. Mom and
Dad couldn't help him with his belt test. Connor was
on his own. He needed to get back his focus and finish
strong.

Connor watched Luke perform Taegeuk Sam Jang.
Luke snapped his dobok with every move. He made
the form look easy. This was not the same Luke who

couldn't remember all the moves to his form last weekend. And Violet showed she was confident and strong with Taegeuk Il Jang.

It was Connor's turn at poomsae again. This was it. His last chance to show the Master Black Belts that he knew Koryeo. Connor ran to his spot, closed his eyes, and took a deep breath. He opened his eyes and breathed out.

Perseverance, thought Connor. *To not give up even when it is hard to keep going.* Connor didn't think about what happened before. Or what would happen next. None of that mattered. What mattered was that he stayed focused on what was happening now. That he made one powerful movement at a time.

His uniform snapped so loud with each block, kick, strike, and punch that everyone in the room probably heard the snapping. Connor made it all the way through his junior black belt form. Without any pauses or mistakes.

The judges nodded their heads and scribbled notes. But no matter what the Master Black Belts thought about his form, Connor knew his Koryeo was perfect this time. Perfect because he gave it everything he had. All his kicks and strikes had *so* much power. Connor stayed focused. And he did his form like he was the only one in the room. Like no one was watching him.

When Connor walked to the back of the room to join the class, Violet and Luke smiled at him. They knew he had nailed his poomsae. Connor looked over at Mom and Dad. They were smiling too. Mom looked so happy that he thought *she* was going to cry.

Connor and Wyatt suited up in their sparring gear. It was time for a rematch. Only this time Connor had a lot more to lose. He needed to prove to the Master Black Belts that he could fight at the poom level. That he was worthy of a junior black belt.

The match started with back-and-forth dollyeo-chagi aimed at the hogu. Connor was in the zone with his roundhouse kicks. It was like he could see what Wyatt was trying to do before he had a chance to do it. But after the first 30 seconds, Wyatt landed two dollyeo-chagi to the chest protector. And Connor only landed one. Connor was down 2–4 in the match.

This time, Connor didn't wait until the end of the round to take a shot at Wyatt's head. He blocked Wyatt's punch-and-roundhouse combination. Connor lifted his right leg straight up in the air. And the ball of his foot came down on the top of Wyatt's head.

Thunk!

The axe kick was good for three points. Connor took the lead 5–4.

Only 30 seconds were left in the match. Wyatt tried to close the lead with nakka-chagi to the head. But Connor was ready for the hook kick this time. He blocked Wyatt's kick and counterattacked with narae-chagi.

Boom! Boom!

The top of Connor's right foot landed on one side of Wyatt's hogu and the top of his left foot on the other side.

The double roundhouse kicks to the chest protector gave Connor four points.

Time was up. Connor had won the match 9–4. He had shown Wyatt that he was the better fighter. Not by a few points either. Connor had crushed Wyatt. Wyatt wouldn't be able to tell the kids in fourth grade that Connor couldn't fight now.

Board breaks were next. And Connor was up first. Wyatt would be holding his boards. *What if he moves the boards?* wondered Connor. He remembered what he had said to Wyatt on the snow obstacle course. "You are *not* a Lion." He had meant to apologize. But he had missed his chance. *Would Wyatt take revenge?* Connor didn't think Wyatt would try to pull off a stunt like that here. Not with three Master Black Belts in the room. *Or would he?* thought Connor.

Connor tried to stop thinking about Wyatt. He had to focus on breaking three wooden boards. He got into fighting stance for his first board break—a spinning hook kick. He moved the board up higher so it was the same height as Wyatt's head. Pivoting on his left foot, Connor spun around backward, letting his head drop down and his foot rise up. He bent his knee and swung his foot across, striking the board with his heel.

Crack!

Next up was the jumping back kick. Wyatt and one of the poom held the board. Launching into the air, Connor spun around, jumped into the air, and threw a donkey kick with his heel.

Crack!

Connor's last board break was a flying side kick. He needed room to run. For this kick, Connor had Wyatt on one side of the board and one of the poom on the other. Connor lined up so he could get a running start. Five rectangular kicking shields were spread out in a row on the floor. They stood between Connor and the wooden board.

He thought about the poster Nick had made. In the drawing, the boy in a dobok wore a half-red and half-black poom belt. Landing this flying side kick would get Connor one step closer to earning his junior black belt.

Connor ran up to the first kicking shield and launched himself into the air. He flew over the five kicking shields and struck the board.

Crack!

Connor flew right through the board and landed on his feet.

Luke broke two boards with a hook kick and a back fist. And Violet broke two with a hammer fist and a front kick.

Once all the board breaks were over, Haley called up the class in groups by rank. Connor lined up, stood at attention, and bowed. He turned around and untied his belt. Connor put his belt in his left hand and turned around to the front of the room.

Master Park tied the half-red and half-black poom belt on Connor. Master Park was serious about Taekwondo and hardly ever smiled. But Connor thought he caught her making a half-smile when she tied on his belt. Connor's smile was so big that it stretched the constellation of freckles on his cheeks.

I'm a junior black belt! thought Connor. *I did it!* Connor's body shook with excitement. He wanted to jump up and down. To scream at the top of his lungs, "I'm a poom!" But this was still Master Park's dojang. And he would follow the tenet of self-control like she had taught him. Even when he had so much to celebrate.

Haley and the other poom passed out belt promotion certificates. Connor shook Haley's hand with his left open palm under his right elbow. The traditional Taekwondo handshake. Haley handed him his certificate. The piece of paper that said he had been promoted to

poom. Connor would get a poom certificate from the
World Taekwondo Headquarters in Korea too.

Connor would *never* forget this day. It was one of the
best days of his life. He couldn't wait to compete in the
tournament as a poom. Connor had trained so hard for
this. To be a junior black belt in the tournament would be
a dream come true.

Luke and Violet passed their belt tests too. Luke
earned his green belt. And Violet, a yellow belt. Luke and
Violet had trained hard, and Connor was proud of them.

After the belt ceremony was over, Connor walked to the back of the room to grab his Taekwondo bag.

A voice behind him said, "Congratulations, Connor."

Connor turned around and stood face-to-face with Wyatt.

"Junior black belt is a big deal," said Wyatt.

Connor stared at Wyatt like he didn't understand what had just happened. *An archenemy doesn't congratulate you*, thought Connor. *Isn't Wyatt mad that I made poom before him?*

Connor didn't thank Wyatt. He didn't say anything at all. It was like Connor knew what he wanted to say but couldn't find the words. By the time he was able to speak again, Wyatt had left the dojang.

Violet fist-bumped Connor. "We did it!" she said. "What did Wyatt say?"

"He congratulated me," said Connor.

"That was nice of him," she said.

Connor hated to admit it. But maybe Violet was right. Maybe Wyatt was nice sometimes.

Violet's parents hugged her.

Luke ran over to Connor. Mom and Dad too. They hugged Connor and Luke. Mom snapped a photo of

Connor and Luke in their new belts. They held up their belt promotion certificates for the photo.

Nick waved the sign at Connor, Violet, and Luke. "The test was just like I drew it on the poster."

They looked at the poster and laughed together.

Haley joined them. "Congrats, Luke and Violet!" She turned to Connor. "Welcome to the poom rank! You earned it."

They took another photo. Nick held the sign in the middle. And Haley, Connor, Violet, and Luke gathered around him.

When they were done taking photos, Master Park waved Connor over.

"Now that you're a poom," said Master Park, "you'll be assisting in the dojang."

"Yes, Ma'am," said Connor.

"Teaching Taekwondo is part of being a black belt," said Master Park. "You really know Taekwondo when you can teach it to other people. Aren't you in an after-school club?"

"Yes, Ma'am," said Connor. "The Infinity Rainbow Club."

"Maybe you could teach a beginner Taekwondo class in your club," said Master Park.

"I'll ask my teacher, Ma'am."

On his way out of the dojang, Connor turned around to bow as usual. But he stopped to look at the Taekwondo tenets on the wall first.

Connor ran his hands along the ends of his poom belt. It was a fresh new belt. Not broken in yet like his red belt with a black stripe. But that would change soon.

The junior black belt test was a real test of his perseverance. A test that had challenged him in every way possible. But Connor had taken on the challenge. Now he stood in the dojang wearing a poom belt. And next Saturday, he would be competing in a tournament as a junior black belt. Because he never gave up.

CHAPTER 10

It snowed again on Tuesday. Connor wanted so badly to escape the classroom. The grinding pencil sharpeners. The squeaking chairs. The tapping pencils. The crumpling papers. Sometimes he felt like his head would explode.

But the school day wasn't all bad for Connor. He loved the breaks in the sensory gym. All the fourth graders with different brains had them at the same time. So Connor got to see Nick and his other friends. In the sensory gym, Connor rode the tube slide into a foam pit. He swung on a swing shaped like a parachute. And he climbed the rock wall.

At outdoor recess, Connor made a snowman with his friends. They had decided at lunch on Monday what they would bring to school if it snowed today. Connor brought a scarf. Violet, a carrot for the nose. Nick, stones for the eyes and mouth. Jasmine, a black hat. And Molly, buttons. Ruby brushed off the snow on their secret stash of sticks in the corner of the playground. And Ruby used two of them for the arms. Connor won one round of the hat toss by landing it on the snowman's head.

At the end of the school day, Connor dug through his backpack looking for his dobok, belt, and kicking target. *Oh no!* Ms. Daisy had said yes when he asked her if he could teach the club a beginner Taekwondo class. And today was the day. But how could he teach without his uniform?

Connor remembered he had taken his uniform and belt downstairs to the kitchen. He was going to put them in his backpack. But he had gone into the basement first to get a kicking target.

When he had gotten back upstairs, he spotted his half-packed lunch box on the kitchen counter. Mom was busy helping Luke get ready for school. Connor must have put down the target somewhere to finish packing his lunch. By the time he was done, he had forgotten all about the Taekwondo equipment.

Connor zipped up his backpack. He wasn't going to find anything he needed in there. Connor asked Mr. Frost if he could go to the front office to call home. Mr. Frost nodded like he always did. Connor walked quickly down the hallway. He knew he would get in trouble for running. His mind raced and his body fidgeted.

"Is everything all right?" asked a woman at a desk in the front office. She went back to staring at her computer screen. Her fingernails stomped on her keyboard. He could never remember her name. But he had had a lot of visits to the front office.

Connor explained what had happened.

"You can use a phone to call home," she said. "Could one of your parents bring your Karate outfit?"

"Taekwondo," Connor corrected her. *Why does everyone think Karate and Taekwondo are the same?* Karate was Japanese. And Taekwondo was Korean. Karate used a lot of hand attacks. And Taekwondo was mostly kicking. Mom never let anyone mix them up when she was around. So Connor had decided he wouldn't either.

Connor really didn't want to bother Mom when he knew she was working from home today. But he made the call. *How can I lead a Taekwondo class for the club without my dobok?*

Keeping an eye on the window, Connor paced back and forth in the front office. It had been ten minutes since he called Mom. She hopped out of her car, threw Connor's Taekwondo bag over her shoulder, and ran through the parking lot.

***

Ms. Daisy stood at the door to the sensory gym in a dobok with a white belt tied around her waist. Connor's mouth dropped open. Ms. Daisy had never said anything about doing Taekwondo before.

"I borrowed a Taekwondo uniform from a friend for today," she said. "This will be my first lesson too. Are you ready to start?"

Connor nodded his head. *As ready as I'm going to be,* he thought.

Ms. Daisy and Connor entered the sensory gym. It didn't have interlocking red and blue foam pads like Connor was used to in the dojang. But the carpeted floor was still comfortable to practice on.

Luke was riding the tube slide into a pit of foam cubes. Nick and Wyatt threw weighted balls at a wall that lit up with blue and red squares. Nick's younger sister, Grace, was riding on a swing shaped like a saucer. Jasmine and her younger sister, Destiny, were climbing on the rock wall. Violet was swinging upside down on the trapeze bar. Ruby and a fifth grader named Matt were climbing across the monkey bars.

"Attention, brilliant buzzing brains!" Ms. Daisy always called the kids in the after-school club by this name. "Let's gather in the space where we normally do balance ball exercises."

Everyone stopped using the equipment. They moved to the large open space in the sensory gym.

"As you know, Connor will be leading us in a Taekwondo lesson today," Ms. Daisy continued. "I'm excited to learn with you. Take it away, Connor!"

Connor walked to the front of the room. He felt weird being up front. *Who am I to be teaching a Taekwondo class? Do I know enough?* He might have passed his junior black belt test. But he wasn't sure if he was ready for this.

After Wyatt joined, the club had thirteen kids. And they were *all* there today, looking at him and waiting for him to start the class. Ms. Daisy too. Connor took a deep breath in and let it out. *Here goes nothing.*

CHAPTER 11

Connor showed everyone how to line up for a Taekwondo class. Wyatt was in the front row on the right. Connor explained that Wyatt's red belt with a black stripe was the highest rank after black belt. Next to Wyatt, Luke wore his green belt. Violet came after Luke. She had her yellow belt. Ms. Daisy was on the far left of the front row in her white belt. And everyone else without a uniform lined up in rows behind them.

"Charyeot." Connor stood at attention with his arms straight at his sides.

The class followed his lead.

"Kyeong-nye." He bowed.

And everyone else did too.

The class ran in a small circle around the sensory gym to warm up before stretching.

Then everyone sat on the floor, their legs spread wide in a large V. Connor was at the front of the room facing the class. Keeping his legs straight, Connor bent forward and grabbed his right foot with both hands.

"We're going to count to ten in Korean while holding each stretch," he said. "Repeat after me. *Hana*, *dul*, *set*, *net*, *taseot*, *yeoseot*, *ilgop*, *yeodeol*, *ahop*, *yeol*." The class repeated the stretch on the other leg. Once they were done with all the stretches, Connor introduced basic stances, blocks, punches, and kicks.

"In Korean," said Connor, "Taekwondo means *way of the hand and foot*. The first kick we're going to learn today is ap-chagi, or front kick."

Violet demonstrated the kick while Connor explained how to do it.

"You raise the knee of your right leg above your waist," said Connor.

Violet stood facing forward. Her right knee pointed straight up in the air.

"Then you snap your foot forward," said Connor. "You should kick with the ball of your foot. Not your toes."

Violet pushed her foot forward with her toes bent back. "Ee-YAH!"

"Did you hear Violet kihap?" asked Connor.

"Does it mean to yell?" asked Destiny.

"Yes, but it's more than shouting," said Connor. "My Taekwondo instructor, Master Park, says kihap means to focus your power. When you kihap, you are forced to breathe out. And that makes your punches and kicks faster and more powerful."

"Does it matter what sound you make?" asked Ruby.

"No," said Connor. "Everyone sounds different when they kihap. And you should be *really* loud when you do it. Hi-YAH!" The sound flooded the sensory gym.

Connor walked around the room helping everyone practice ap-chagi. Nick had a good snap for his front kick. Connor wondered if Haley had taught him how to do it.

Connor decided it was time to teach poomsae. The form for beginners is Taegeuk Il Jang. The same form Violet had to know for her test to become a yellow belt.

"Watch me do the opening of Taegeuk Il Jang," said Connor. "And then you can try the moves together. The color belts know it already, so you can follow them."

Connor stood at the front of the room with his back to the class. The sensory gym didn't have mirrors covering the front wall like the dojang. So Connor couldn't see the class behind him.

He did a lower block and took a step. But then he froze. He just stood there. It was like the sparring match he lost against Wyatt. Only this time, it wasn't that he knew what move he wanted to make but couldn't do it. He didn't even remember what he was doing. It was like he forgot that he was in the middle of a poomsae. And that he was running a Taekwondo class. What if he froze up at the tournament on Saturday too? Would he forget Koryeo like he did during the belt test? Would he freeze in a Taekwondo match against a Titan?

"Are you all right, Connor?" asked Ms. Daisy.

Connor turned around to face the class. They looked worried. And that was when he realized that he had zoned out doing Taegeuk Il Jang.

How could I forget the yellow belt form? Connor had just done Koryeo for his junior black belt test. And it was a much harder form to remember with advanced moves. And now he couldn't even do the poomsae for a complete beginner to Taekwondo. Only, he *knew* the moves. He just couldn't stay focused long enough to do them.

"Excuse me, Sir," said Wyatt.

"Yes, Wyatt." Connor was shocked that Wyatt called him Sir. This was the first time anyone had ever called him that. But now that he was a poom, the color belts in Master Park's dojang would call him that too.

"Should I come up in the front row so that everyone can see Taegeuk Il Jang?" asked Wyatt. "We could do the poomsae together."

Wyatt made it sound like he was helping the class. But Connor knew that this was Wyatt's way of helping him. It would probably be easier for Connor to focus if he had someone else doing the poomsae next to him. Connor thought about how he had treated Wyatt. "You're *not* a Lion," he had said when Wyatt wouldn't spar with Connor on the snow obstacle course. Connor wished he hadn't been so mean to Wyatt.

"Yes, Wyatt," said Connor. "Come to the front row, please."

"Yes, Sir!" Wyatt ran to the front of the room.

Wyatt was on Connor's left. Connor was able see him out of the corner of his eye. They did the first few moves of Taegeuk II Jang together. Low block, step, punch. Turn. Low block, step, punch. And the class repeated the sequence. Connor didn't zone out this time. He kept his focus. And Connor felt better having Wyatt at his side in case he needed help again.

No one in the club said anything or laughed at Connor for freezing up. Not all of them had ADHD like Connor did. But most of them knew what it was like to lose their focus.

At the end of class, Connor asked Luke to get the kicking target. *Too bad Ace isn't here*, thought Connor. Luke held the paddle. Connor threw dollyeo-chagi at it.

BOOM!

It sounded like thunder. But not quite as loud as Mom's roundhouse kick. Jasmine and Matt jumped back.

Connor and Luke explained the potential and kinetic energy of dollyeo-chagi like Mom had taught them. Connor could tell that Ms. Daisy was impressed. She probably wasn't expecting them to talk about the physics of Taekwondo.

The group lined up to kick the target. Connor made sure everyone had a good fighting stance before they kicked. Bouncing on their toes. Fists up near their heads.

The clapping noise of the clamshell paddle coming together filled the sensory gym. *Ms. Daisy has a mean kick*, thought Connor. And Destiny and Grace had a lot of power in their kicks for second graders.

Connor had everyone line up and bow. And he dismissed the class. He took a deep breath in and out. His first class was a success. Everyone said they had fun. They even begged Ms. Daisy to let them do it again. Connor was proud of himself. He had made it all the way through teaching his first class. It wasn't easy. Nothing about Taekwondo was easy. But the more he practiced, the more he was able to focus his mind and body.

The club had free time while waiting for their parents to pick them up.

Connor picked up a slam ball. The tiny bumps on it felt funny on his fingers. He hurled it against the wall. *Smash!*

Nick bent down and grabbed a slam ball too. "It was a fun Taekwondo class." He threw the ball near the spot Connor had already hit. *Smash!*

"Thanks." Connor lunged to scoop up another slam ball. "The first time is always hard. But I want to teach more classes and get better at it." He launched the ball at the wall. *Smash!*

"Nick and Grace!" Ms. Daisy yelled. "Your mom's here."

"I hope you teach the club again," said Nick. "I'll definitely be there."

Nick left with his mom and Grace.

Wyatt joined Connor at the wall. "This is my favorite station." Wyatt scooped up a slam ball. "You don't have to think about anything. You just throw the ball at the wall." And he launched it. *Smash!*

"Yep," Connor grabbed a ball. Maybe it wasn't too late to apologize to Wyatt. "Sorry about what happened at recess last week. I shouldn't have said you weren't a Lion. And thanks for helping me with Taegeuk Il Jang. Sometimes I freeze up in the middle of a form." He threw the ball at the wall. *Smash!*

Wyatt bent down to pick up another ball. "Yeah, me too. I've been having trouble learning the moves for Koryeo. That's why I wasn't ready to test for poom." He hurled the ball at the wall. *Smash!*

Connor paused with a ball in his hand. "I thought you didn't test because you switched your dojang." He thought back to the Taekwondo classes last week. He didn't think Wyatt was that good at Koryeo. But he didn't know Wyatt was struggling that much. "I had no idea."

"I have dyscalculia," said Wyatt.

"You do?" Connor looked over at Wyatt.

Wyatt nodded.

"Yeah," said Wyatt, "I have trouble doing simple math problems in my head. I forget how many kicks, blocks, or punches I need to do or what order they're in for my forms."

"I have ADHD," said Connor. "Forms are the hardest part of Taekwondo for me."

"Connor and Luke!" yelled Ms. Daisy. "Your mom's here."

"Maybe we could practice Koryeo together sometime," said Connor.

"That would be awesome," said Wyatt.

Connor threw the ball he still had in his hand. *Smash!* And he left the sensory gym with Mom and Luke.

"I see that you're getting along with Wyatt," Mom said to Connor and smiled. Mom had seen Connor battle it out with Wyatt in tournaments. And in the sparring match at the junior black belt test on Saturday too.

"I thought he was your archenemy." Luke punched and kicked in the air.

"He was," said Connor. "But now he's a Lion." Connor decided that Violet was right. "And he seems nice."

CHAPTER 12

On Thursday, the Lions had their final team practice before the tournament. Master Park assigned Connor and Wyatt as partners for the hogu drills.

They stood across from each other with their arms hanging wide around their chest protectors, waiting for instructions from Master Park. Instead of using light contact like they usually did for hogu drills, they would be kicking each other with full power. For extra protection, they wore double hogu.

"I feel like a blueberry." Connor wore a double layer of blue hogu. His middle was twice as big as it normally was. The second chest protector wrapped around the first and tied loosely like a big shoelace on his back.

Wyatt laughed, shaking his double layer of red hogu. "I guess that makes me a cherry."

Connor laughed too.

"Attention!" said Master Park. "For the first hogu drill, move in a straight line across the dojang with your partner."

Haley and another poom demonstrated while Master Park explained how to do the drill.

"Take turns attacking with dollyeo-chagi," said Master Park. "Targets, make sure you keep your arms loose to the side and out of the way."

Haley's leg moved up and down so fast it was as if she was bouncing her leg off the floor to hit her opponent's hogu. Her roundhouse kicks were powerful.

"When you're the target," Master Park continued, "keep moving your feet so your partner has to adjust their dollyeo-chagi based on your body position. Do not try to block your opponent's kick. You should take two turns as a target and two turns as a kicker. Then, take off your hogu and stretch while you wait for the rest of the class to finish. Shijak!"

The class began the drill.

"Do you want to kick first?" asked Connor.

"Sure," said Wyatt.

Connor slid his way backward across the padded floor while Wyatt pounded Connor's hogu.

"KYA!"

Thud!

"KYA!"

Thud!

With all the hits, Connor had to fight to keep his balance. But the double hogu protected him from bruises. As he moved backward step by step, Connor shifted where he landed his back foot to change the angle of the target.

When they made it across the dojang, Wyatt sucked air in to catch his breath.

Then, it was Connor's turn.

"Hi-YAH!"

Thud!

"Hi-YAH!"

Thud!

Connor banged the hogu just as hard as Wyatt. All the way across the dojang again. When he finished, Connor took deep breaths in and out.

Connor and Wyatt repeated the drill a second time. Taking turns kicking again. They finished the drill first.

"Are you ready for the tournament on Saturday?" asked Connor, while Wyatt untied Connor's hogu. Connor had trouble tying and untying one hogu. But he couldn't do it at all with two.

"Yeah," said Wyatt. "But it's going to be strange fighting against the Titans instead of with them this time."

Connor pulled off the first hogu, and Wyatt began untying the other one.

"In the lightweight class for poom," said Wyatt, "you'll probably fight Back Kick Jack and Tornado Ollie."

Connor laughed. "Back Kick Jack and Tornado Ollie? Did you just make up those names?" Connor took off his other hogu and began untying Wyatt's.

"Nope," said Wyatt. "The Titans have nicknames for all the fighters. Back Kick Jack never loses. Nobody likes fighting him. You have to watch out for his jumping back kicks."

Wyatt took off his first hogu. Connor began untying the second one.

"I'll remember that on Saturday," said Connor. "But I hope I won't be fighting Back Kick Jack. Tornado Ollie must be good at dolgae-chagi."

"Really good," said Wyatt. "But your axe kicks are just as good as his tornado kicks."

Wyatt removed his other hogu. Connor and Wyatt sat down on the padded floor and began stretching their legs.

"I kind of want a nickname too," said Connor.

"The Titans gave you one," said Wyatt.

"Seriously?" asked Connor.

Wyatt nodded. "Axe Kick Connor. It was my idea."

"I like it!" Connor bent his knees and brought his feet together into a butterfly pose. He held his feet with his hands and used his elbows to push down on his legs. "Do *you* have a nickname?"

"Yeah." Wyatt got into butterfly pose too. "You know my last name is Cook, right?"

Connor nodded.

"Cook the Hook."

Connor laughed. "That's perfect! You have a mean nakka-chagi."

When everyone was done with the drill, they practiced poomsae with their partners. Connor and Wyatt did Koryeo side by side. They stayed together in the beginning through the double knife hand blocks and the double side kicks. And the front kicks and the low knife hand blocks too. But then Wyatt lost track of the pattern.

"I'm sorry," said Wyatt. "I messed up again." He held his head in his hands. His face reminded Connor of Luke when he forgot Taegeuk Sam Jang. And that was exactly what Connor had wanted to do when he froze up in the middle of Koryeo during his junior black belt test.

"When I have trouble with my forms," said Connor, "I think about how it takes perseverance to get them right." He pointed to the tenet on the wall. "You saw me forget the moves to Koryeo twice at my belt test. Thinking about perseverance is what helped me get through it the third time. To not give up even when it was hard to keep going."

Wyatt nodded. Connor and Wyatt got into tongmilgi-junbi—the log pushing posture—and ran through Koryeo together again. Connor could tell that Wyatt was unsure about what to do next a few times. But this time they made it all the way through Koryeo.

Then they did it again, even better than before.

Master Park asked Connor and Wyatt to stay after practice to talk to her.

"You both looked strong and powerful with dollyeo-chagi for the hogu drill." Master Park turned toward Connor. "Your Koryeo looks very good." She looked at Wyatt. "You're improving your form too. I'm glad to see you two getting along so well. I look forward to seeing what you will do together as a team in the tournament on Saturday."

"Yes, Ma'am," said Connor and Wyatt at the same time.

Connor bowed before leaving the dojang. *Master Park said strong and powerful!* thought Connor. That was huge coming from her. Master Park never said anything she didn't mean. Connor felt stronger and more powerful than he had ever felt before. He was so ready for this tournament. Connor had waited so long to step into a ring as a poom.

CHAPTER 13

On Saturday, the Lions had the Three Rivers Taekwondo Tournament in a college gym. Connor had been competing in this tournament for the past five years. Mom and Dad had always come to watch him and Luke. Just like they did today.

The gym was about four times the size of Master Park's dojang. In the middle of the gym, interlocking blue foam squares formed eight large sparring rings. Around the blue squares, red foam squares covered most of the floor.

The rings were used for sparring matches and poomsae. Long judges' tables covered with white cloth ran along the side of the rings. In the back of the gym an award table was stacked with gold, silver, and bronze medals.

Nick had made a new poster that looked like a comic with figures sparring and doing poomsae. At the top of the poster it said, "Go Lions!" Connor gave Nick a fist bump before he joined his team to warm up.

The Lions and Titans staked out their warm-up areas in different corners of the gym. Mom and Dad sat in the bleachers near Nick, his parents, and Grace. Violet's parents, her grandma, and Bo were also with them.

For the tournament, color belts and pooms had two 90-second rounds of sparring with a 30-second rest between rounds. Haley fought a poom in one ring. And in a ring next to her, Wyatt fought an opponent of his rank. Connor, Violet, and Luke sat in a space on the floor for competitors only. They had a good view of Haley and Wyatt's matches.

"Go Lions!" yelled Connor in Wyatt's direction.

"Are you cheering for Haley or Wyatt?" asked Violet.

"Both," said Connor.

"Really?" said Violet. "Isn't Wyatt your rival?"

"Wyatt's not his archenemy anymore," said Luke.

"Oh really?" Violet looked at Connor. "What changed?"

"Did you see that spinning hook kick he threw?" asked Connor. Wyatt had landed it on his opponent's head. *Cook the Hook strikes again*, thought Connor. Spinning kicks to the head were worth five points. The most points you could score in one hit. "We need more fighters like him."

"I'm serious," said Violet. "What changed?" She wasn't going to let him off easy.

"Okay, I was wrong about Wyatt," said Connor. "I shouldn't have been mean to him just because he used to be on the Titans."

"And?" she asked.

"And you were right," said Connor. "He seems nice. Is that what you wanted to hear?"

"Yes, definitely that part about me being right." Violet smiled.

Boom!

"Whoa!" yelled Connor. "Did you see that?"

"Yeah, but what kind of kick did Haley do?" asked Violet.

"Dolgae-chagi or tornado kick," said Connor. "It's a 360-degree jumping roundhouse kick. Haley spun around on her front foot. But then instead of throwing her kick with her back leg, she switched legs and threw a roundhouse kick in the air."

"She moved so fast she looked like a tornado!" said Violet.

"We need to practice more tornado kicks," said Luke. "I want to be able to score like that too."

"I want to learn to spar," said Violet.

"I started when I was a yellow belt," said Connor.

"Me too," said Luke.

"I'll be in full sparring gear for the next tournament," said Violet. "The Titans better watch out."

Connor looked at the clock on the gym wall. He needed to start warming up for his first match. Connor left Violet and Luke to get ready on his own. *Time to focus*, thought Connor.

He jogged in a circle around an open space on the gym floor. Connor couldn't believe that today would be his first match ever as a poom. He had been looking forward to this day for as long as he could remember.

Connor ran through his stretches and warm-up kicks, counting in Korean in his head. He got into fighting stance and threw air kicks at an imaginary opponent. His mind raced through all the times he had lost his focus in matches.

Connor looked around the room at his teammates fighting in rings and his parents and friends watching in the stands. *I have to fight Back Kick Jack in my first match as a junior black belt*, thought Connor. *So much pressure.* At least he knew to watch out for dwi-chagi. He took a deep breath in and out as he walked to the sparring ring.

"Your first match as a poom," said Master Park. "Are you ready?"

"Yes, Ma'am," Connor said. But he wasn't sure if he was ready. What if he froze up during his first match as a junior black belt? What if he had waited all this time and had trained for so many years just to lose his focus when it really mattered?

The referee pointed to the center of the ring. "Chung!" he said.

Connor stepped up to where the referee pointed. He wore the blue side of his hogu.

The referee pointed to the space across from Connor. "Hong!"

Jack entered the center of the ring in a red hogu.

In full sparring gear, they carried their helmets tucked under their left arms.

"Charyeot," the referee said.

Connor and his opponent stood at attention with their arms by their sides.

"Kyeong-nye," the referee said.

They faced each other and bowed. Then they put on their headgear.

The referee lunged with his left leg. His open hand near his ear swung down between Connor and Jack. "Junbi!" The referee waited until they were in fighting stance.

The referee slid his left leg backward. He brought both of his hands together in front of him. "Shijak!" And the match began.

Master Park watched Connor and his opponent like a lion from outside the ring.

Connor made the first move. He faked dollyeo-chagi to the side of Jack's hogu and attacked with naeryeo-chagi aimed at Jack's head. But Jack didn't fall for the fake roundhouse kick. And he blocked Connor's axe kick.

Connor and Jack switched their legs back and forth, sliding around the ring on the balls of their feet. Sweat from under Connor's helmet ran down the side of his face.

Jack switched his legs again. And right when Connor switched his legs, Jack attacked with dollyeo-chagi. "CHA!"

Boom!

The roundhouse kick hit the side of Connor's hogu. Jack spun to his right, looking over his right shoulder. He donkey kicked backward. "CHA!"

Boom!

Dwi-chagi landed in the middle of Connor's hogu and knocked him over.

The crowd roared. But Connor bounced right off the foam-padded floor and was on his feet again fighting. The roundhouse kick was worth two points. And the back kick, four points.

The first 90-second round ended with Jack in the lead 6–0.

In their corners, Connor and Jack had a 30-second break with their coaches.

"Keep your head up," said Master Park. "It's always hard to stay in the fight when you're behind. But you can do this."

The final 90-second round started with a lot of switches and failed dollyeo-chagi.

Then Back Kick Jack threw another dwi-chagi. "CHA!"

Boom!

Connor took the hit and stood on his feet this time. Jack got four more points for the back kick. He was winning 10–0.

Perseverance, thought Connor. *To not give up even when it is hard to keep going.* Connor was not going to end his first match as a poom with no points. *I'm better than that!*

Connor threw dolgae-chagi. But Jack blocked the tornado kick. Connor tried narae-chagi. But Jack blocked the double roundhouse kicks too. Then Connor punched Jack in the hogu. "Ki-YAH!"

Boom!

And Connor threw an axe kick at Jack's head. "Ki-YAH!"

Boom!

And just like that, Connor had four points. Time was up. Jack had won 10–4. But Connor ended strong.

Connor couldn't believe he didn't freeze up like he had feared. He had kept his head up and stayed in the fight like Master Park had taught him. But that wasn't enough to win. Wyatt had warned him that Back Kick Jack never lost. But he was a much better fighter than Connor had expected.

Connor wasn't done yet. A poom wouldn't give up that easily. He had another fight later. Connor couldn't wait to get back in the ring. To show everyone why *he* had earned the rank of junior black belt.

CHAPTER 14

As a team, the Lions were having a good day at the tournament. Haley and Wyatt both won their sparring matches and advanced to the next round. Haley won the next two matches. She took the gold for poom belts in her weight class. Wyatt lost his second match. He finished in fourth place for red belts with black stripes in his division.

Luke lost his first sparring match but won his second. He got a bronze medal for placing third for green belts in his weight class. Violet won a silver medal for yellow belts in poomsae.

It was time for Connor's second sparring match. He stood in the ring face-to-face with Tornado Ollie. Connor remembered what Wyatt had said about Ollie's mean dolgae-chagi.

Sure enough, Tornado Ollie made the first move with a tornado kick. "AH!"

He wasn't messing around. But Connor blocked it.

Connor counterattacked with a dollyeo-chagi to the head. "Hi-YAH!"

But Ollie blocked Connor's roundhouse kick. The round continued with switches back and forth. And more failed roundhouse kicks on both sides. No one scored in the first 90-second round.

The fighters took a 30-second break in their corners with the coaches.

"Keep your focus," said Master Park. "And read your opponent. You got this."

The final 90-second round started. Ollie came in fast, throwing a punch—"AH!"—and a roundhouse kick—"AH!" But Connor blocked both of them.

Connor and Ollie went back and forth throwing roundhouse kicks.

"AH!" yelled Ollie.

Boom!

He landed dollyeo-chagi on Connor's hogu.

"Hi-YAH!" yelled Connor.

Boom!

He scored with a roundhouse kick too.

The score was tied up at 2–2.

But not for long. Tornado Ollie swirled around like a tornado. "AH!"

Boom!

Dolgae-chagi landed on Connor's hogu. The tornado kick gave Ollie four points. He was winning 6–2.

But Connor was not giving up. He swung his leg up high and came down on Ollie's head. "Hi-YAH!"

Thunk!

The crowd cheered. Connor landed naeryeo-chagi to the head. The axe kick was worth three points. But Connor still trailed behind 6–5.

Time was ticking down. Connor felt like he was on fire. Sweat dripped from his forehead. *Perseverance,* thought Connor. *To not give up even when it is hard to keep going.* Connor was *so* tired. But he slid back and forth, reacting to Ollie. Connor blocked another dollyeo-chagi. He couldn't give up now. He was only down by one point. Connor threw dollyeo-chagi. "Hi-YAH!"

But Ollie batted the roundhouse kick away. And time on the clock ran out. The match was over. Tornado Ollie won 6–5.

Ollie put out his hand for a traditional Taekwondo handshake. And Connor shook it. If only he had more time, he could've beaten Ollie. Just one more dollyeo-chagi on the hogu. Competing with other black belts at a tournament was a dream for Connor. It was everything he

had ever wanted. Just being in the gym surrounded by other black belts felt amazing.

Connor knew that the odds were against him winning today. After all, he had just got his junior black belt last week. He didn't expect to be the best in his first tournament at a new rank. But he had hoped he would win one match.

Connor didn't win either of his fights. But he didn't lose them either, even though the tournament would record the matches as losses for him. Connor didn't give up or lose his focus. He stuck out the matches to the very end. And the second match was close.

Connor walked out of the ring, swinging his helmet in his hand. Luke, Haley, Wyatt, and his other teammates cheered for him. Nick waved a poster in the bleachers too. When Connor looked up in the stands, Mom and Dad smiled back at him. And if Ace were here, he'd be jumping up and down like a mascot cheering Connor on.

Connor had given his fights everything he had and more. And that made him a winner. He was proud of himself. Connor grabbed the end of his junior black belt and rubbed it. The crisp new belt wasn't broken in yet. Connor knew this tournament was just the first of many he would have as a poom. Axe Kick Connor would be back again for the next one. *Bring it on!*

CONNOR'S GUIDE TO TAEKWONDO

Junior Belt Rank (Belt colors can vary by dojang):

White belt—10th gup (beginner)
Yellow belt—8th gup
Yellow belt with green stripe—7th gup
Green belt—6th gup
Green belt with blue stripe—5th gup
Blue belt—4th gup
Blue belt with red stripe—3rd gup
Red belt—2nd gup
Red belt with black stripe—1st gup
Junior black belt—1st poom

Korean terms:

ahnjoe: sit
ap-chagi: front kick
charyeot: attention
chung: blue
dobok: uniform

dojang: a place to train in martial arts
dolgae-chagi: tornado kick
dollyeo-chagi: roundhouse kick
dwi-chagi: back kick
gup: rank or degree
hogu: chest protector
hong: red
jong yul: line up
junbi: ready
kihap: to focus your power in a yell
kyeong-nye: bow
kyeorugi: sparring
naeryeo-chagi: axe kick
nakka-chagi: hook kick
narae-chagi: double kicks
paro: as you were
poom: junior black belt
poomsae: forms
shijak: begin
tongmilgi-junbi: log pushing posture
yeop-chagi: side kick

JEN MALIA is a professor of English and the creative writing coordinator at Norfolk State University. Originally from Pittsburgh, she currently lives in Virginia Beach with her husband and three kids. Jen has written for the *New York Times*, the *Washington Post*, *New York Magazine*, *Woman's Day*, *Glamour*, *Self*, and others. Jen is the author of The Infinity Rainbow Club series and *Too Sticky! Sensory Issues with Autism*. Jen was diagnosed with ASD in her late thirties and has three neurodivergent kids with different combinations of ASD, ADHD, OCD, dyslexia, and dysgraphia.

PETER FRANCIS lives in England, where for over twenty years he has diligently created fresh, bright illustrations for both children's publishing and British television. His artwork is playful, thoughtful, and engaging. When not frantically sketching away, he explores castles, immerses himself in nature, paints, laughs, and (if time) sleeps!